with
all good wishes

Ruth Sanderson

~ 1991 ~

The Enchanted Wood

AN ORIGINAL FAIRY TALE

by Ruth Sanderson

LITTLE, BROWN AND COMPANY

BOSTON TORONTO LONDON

First Edition

Library of Congress Cataloging-in-Publication Data

Sanderson, Ruth.
    The enchanted wood : an original fairy tale / by Ruth Sanderson. —
1st ed.
        p.   cm.
    Summary: Three princes go on a quest to the Heart of the World to
save their drought-ravaged kingdom.
    ISBN 0-316-77018-3
    [1. Fairy tales.]   I. Title.
PZ8.S253   En   1991
[E] — dc20   90-45096

10 9 8 7 6 5 4 3 2 1

HR

Published simultaneously in Canada
by Little, Brown & Company (Canada) Limited

Printed in the United States of America

Paintings done in oil on canvas
Calligraphy by Judythe Sieke

To my husband, Ken,
my daughters, Morgan and Whitney,
and my mother, Victoria Sanderson

$\mathcal{L}$ong ago, there was a land green and fair. Its gently rolling hills were covered with orchards, wide pastures, and rich farmlands. Its forests echoed with bird song and were filled with deer and wild boar, pheasant and hare. The king of this land was wise and just, and the queen was loved and honored by all.

But then a sad day came to the kingdom, when the queen died after giving

birth to her third son. The king grieved for his queen, and though he loved his sons, he could no longer find joy in life. The land seemed to share the king's grief. Each year after the queen's death, a little less rain fell on the kingdom. The crops grew sparse, the fruit was eaten by worms, and the animals became thin and weak. Finally, the land was gripped with a terrible drought. Streams dried up, crops withered, and fields turned to dust. The king grew desperate, for his subjects were on the verge of starvation.

One day the king called his sons to him. "A legend says that if a man of royal blood and noble purpose can find the Heart of the World, his purpose will be magically achieved. Surely, our need to end this terrible drought is such a noble cause."

"I have heard this legend," said Edmund, the eldest prince. "The stories also say that the Heart of the World lies beyond the mountains, in the Enchanted Wood." This quest sounded like a great hunt to Edmund, for he loved good sport above all.

"I, too, remember those tales," said Owen, the second prince. "The stories also say that the Enchanted Wood is a place of great danger, and that no one has ever escaped from its deadly snares." Owen was known far and wide as a great warrior and loved a

good fight no matter what the cause.

Galen, the king's youngest son, spoke last. "I would gladly go on this worthy quest," he said. Galen had great admiration for his older brothers and wanted to show that he could be as brave as they were.

Edmund and Owen smiled and winked at each other, for Galen was still a lad and had no experience in hunting or in battle.

The king looked at each of his sons and spoke once more: "I am too old and weary and have no heart to rule much longer. If one of you succeeds in this quest, he will deserve to become king in my stead."

Since Edmund was the eldest, he would be the first to attempt the quest. He set out the next morning and crossed the northern mountains. After three days of hard traveling, he saw the Enchanted Wood looming darkly before him, bordered by high, thorn-covered walls. A great iron gate barred the path, and Edmund reined in his horse. An old woman came out of a stone hut to greet him.

"I have been expecting you, king's son," she said.

"What do you mean, old hag?" said Edmund with disdain. "What could you know of princely affairs?"

"I know much," said the wise woman softly. "And I am bound, as gatekeeper of the Enchanted Wood, to give you this warning:

Be true to the quest, at any cost;
Stray from the path, and you will be lost.

"Open the gate quickly, old woman," demanded Edmund, "for I am the greatest huntsman in the kingdom and need no advice from the likes of you." Bowing humbly, the wise woman fitted a silver key in the lock and slowly pushed open the gate.

Edmund spurred his horse into the Enchanted Wood without a backward glance. He had not gone far when he spied something moving through the trees. It was a pure white stag of marvelous proportions. Edmund could not resist a chance to hunt such a magnificent creature. He jumped from his horse, and taking up his bow, he ran from the path in pursuit of the perfect stag.

A fortnight later, when Edmund had not returned, the king's second son eagerly set out for the Enchanted Wood. "I will succeed in this quest and bring my foolish brother back with me," he boasted. Owen was sure he would find and capture the Heart of the World and command it to end the drought.

Owen, too, was met by the wise woman when he arrived at the gate. She spoke the same warning to him:

Be true to the quest, at any cost;
Stray from the path, and you will be lost.

Owen just laughed at her words. "I am the greatest warrior in the kingdom, and I am not afraid of any danger the Wood might hold." Silently, the wise woman opened the gate for the king's second son. He proudly entered the Enchanted Wood on his prancing charger, thinking what a grand picture he must make with his jeweled sword and shining coat of mail.

Owen had not traveled far before he, too, was tempted to leave the path. For soon a knight in black armor appeared in the forest a short distance away.

"Who are you, and what king do you serve?" Owen demanded.

The black knight did not speak, nor did he threaten the prince in any way. Instead he remained among the trees, keeping pace with Owen and mocking him with stony silence. Owen held his head high and tried to ignore the knight, but he became more and more angry at the black knight's insolence.

Finally, Owen could stand it no longer. With a battle cry, he charged into the Wood after the impertinent knight.

When another fortnight passed with no sign of Owen or Edmund, the king's youngest son, Galen, became determined to follow his brothers. He begged his father to let him go on the quest. The king was very reluctant, for he did not know what fate his other sons had met. "I will find the Heart of the World and my brothers as well," Galen promised. But the king would not relent. Finally, one night, Galen managed to slip out of the castle unseen.

Galen, like his brothers, heard the wise woman's warning at the gate:

> *Be true to the quest, at any cost;*
> *Stray from the path, and you will be lost.*

But instead of demanding that she open the gate, Galen dismounted from his horse. "If you are willing, kind woman, my horse needs a rest," he said, "and so do I."

"Put the beast in back and give him some fodder," she instructed the king's son. "Then you can join us for dinner. My daughter Rose can make herbs and wild roots taste like a feast."

Galen did as she told him, though at home a commoner would have been beaten for telling a prince to tend his own horse.

After dinner, Rose asked Galen, "What do you seek in the Enchanted Wood?" Galen spoke of the suffering of the people and how he would ask the Heart of the World to end the drought. "And if there is a way," he added, "I will find my brothers. For my father will surely die of grief if I do not." Galen looked up at the wise woman's daughter. "You face a most difficult task," she said. "I hope you will succeed."

The next morning, Galen shouldered his pack, choosing to leave his horse in the care of the wise woman. He was surprised when Rose came out of the hut with a waterskin and travel bag. "Please take me with you," she said, "for I may be able to help you on this quest."

Galen looked to Rose's mother, who simply nodded in consent. He said to Rose, "I trust that your mother, being a wise woman, can see things that others cannot. Since your mother gives her permission, I welcome your company." Rose smiled and took her place at Galen's side.

The wise woman unlocked the gate for Galen and her daughter. She then placed

the key on its chain around Rose's neck. "For luck," she said. Galen thought that Rose looked more beautiful wearing that simple chain than did all the ladies of the court with their finest jewels.

Rose had no trouble matching Galen's swift pace. The Enchanted Wood was a gray, bleak place, unnaturally still and quiet. Its trees were strangely twisted and gnarled, and thorny brambles grew thickly on all sides. The two travelers walked for hours watching pale mists swirling into fantastic shapes that seemed almost alive. Finally, the mists grew thicker and thicker, until it was so difficult to see they were guided only by the low stone wall that bordered the narrow path.

Suddenly, Galen and Rose heard a commotion in the Wood. They stopped and peered in, straining to see through the fog. Then, with one graceful bound, a magnificent white stag leapt over the path in front of them and disappeared into the forest on the other side. Close behind appeared Edmund, bow in hand, haggard and out of breath. He lurched onto the path.

"Edmund, wait!" cried Galen, but it was too late. His brother had leapt off the path again, before Galen could make a move to stop him. Edmund followed the stag's trail and was soon swallowed by the fog.

"I must go after him!" Galen declared. But Rose held him back, saying, "No, my prince! Remember the warning. If you leave the path, you too will become enchanted, and all will be lost."

Galen looked sadly after his brother and knew that she was right. With slow, reluctant steps, he continued down the path.

In a few hours the mist that had covered the forest began to clear, and Galen and Rose stopped to rest. Galen forced himself to eat although he had no appetite. As the two sat on the ground, they felt a faint vibration, then heard a drumming sound,

which quickly grew louder and louder. Rose and Galen were nearly knocked from the path when a riderless, wild-eyed horse galloped by. "Owen's charger!" cried Galen. "But what has become of my brother?"

A clash of metal upon metal sounded in the Wood. Suddenly Owen and the black knight emerged from the trees, locked in endless combat. Owen looked worse than Edmund had, for he bled from many wounds. Galen drew his sword, ready to run to his brother's side. Then he hesitated and turned to Rose. "This is indeed an evil wood," declared Galen. "I cannot risk setting foot off this path, even to help my own brothers." Slowly Galen put away his sword and turned from his brother, saying grimly, "Let us go on."

Galen was lost in sorrow at the fate of his two brothers, and he wondered what doom the Enchanted Wood held for him. He felt his feet grow heavier with each step. After a while, he spoke. "I cannot understand this enchanted place. My brothers were tempted by what they love most, hunting and fighting. But where, then, is my temptation?"

"Don't you see?" said Rose. "What you love most is your brothers, so you wanted to leave the road to help them. Instead, you chose to stay on the path and remain

true to your purpose to help all the people of the kingdom."

As she spoke, Galen noticed that all around them the forest had begun to change. Trees that were stunted and leafless a moment before began to branch and bud. Blossoms appeared on lifeless thorn bushes. Pale green points sprang up out of the moldy earth, turning into wildflowers that spread over the ground like a carpet being unrolled for a king. Watching the forest change, Galen felt lighter and less burdened. Then, as they walked around a bend, the path came to an end in a sunny, open glade.

There, in the center of the clearing, stood a wonderful tree, the like of which they had never seen. They understood that here was the Heart of the World, as old as the earth itself. Three enormous trunks intertwined and grew as one, in perfect harmony of form. The great tree's crown of leaves shone red-gold in the light, and a spring poured from between its roots, forming a small pool that sparkled in the sun.

Without hesitation, Galen cupped his hands and filled them. He drank deeply of the water from the Heart of the World, and then he said, "It is my solemn wish that, from this time on, there will always be enough rain for a bountiful harvest throughout the land." Immediately dark rain clouds began to form overhead, blowing southward toward the parched fields of the kingdom. Galen had fulfilled the quest.

Then Rose stepped forward. She took the key to the Enchanted Wood from around her neck, and holding it in her outstretched hand, she chanted:

> *The Enchanted Wood has lost its power*
> *To lure and tempt; for in this hour*
> *The quest is won, the land renewed.*
> *This Heart's not meant for mortal view!*

Then Rose threw the key into the pool, and before Galen could express his surprise, the air around them began to shimmer. As they backed away from the Heart of the World, it faded and soon disappeared from sight. Even the pool was empty and dry.

Rose answered his questioning look. "For generations my ancestors have been bound as keepers of the gate. We have warned many, many men who were lured by the power that the Heart of the World can grant. We knew that unless they were pure of heart, they would stray from the path and meet their doom. Yet we were bound to let them try, knowing that only one was destined to succeed."

"Surely any man could succeed with your help," interrupted Galen.

"I have not offered my help to any other," said Rose. "And now, I have also freed my mother and myself from the binding of the Wood. For it is no longer enchanted and will never again need a gatekeeper."

Galen realized what Rose had done: "Now no one else will be doomed to failure." His brothers and the other men would be freed. The young prince seized Rose's hand and hurried back to the road. It was not long before they came upon Owen. He sat on a tree stump, holding his broken sword and looking ashamed. The trees around him bore many hack marks, but there was no black knight to be seen. He was truly glad to hear that Galen had fulfilled the quest. "You deserve to be king," Owen told him.

Farther on they met Edmund coming toward them on the path. Though he was thin and weak, Edmund embraced his brother. "I was a fool to let my love of the hunt come before all else," he said.

Hand in hand, Rose and Galen returned with his two brothers to the gate. The wise woman was waiting there and thanked them for freeing her. She turned to Galen and said, "It seems my daughter chose wisely. I hoped you were the one who would win the Heart of the World."

The king's joy knew no bounds when all three of his sons returned from the Enchanted Wood, and he welcomed the gentle and beautiful Rose and her wise mother. The rain quickly brought back life to the parched fields, and that winter there was bread to spare in the kingdom. The king held a great feast to honor Galen

and Rose, and the long-absent sounds of music and merriment filled the castle. With the coming of the new year, the fruit of the orchards grew sweet and the pastures became lush and green. Birds sang in meadow and forest, where deer and wild boar, pheasant and hare, thrived in abundance.

In time, Galen became king and asked Rose to become his queen. Together they ruled happily and wisely for the rest of their days. Songs were sung and tales were told of the great quest so that the winning of the Heart of the World in the Enchanted Wood might never be forgotten.

Naamah and the Ark at Night

a lullaby by SUSAN CAMPBELL BARTOLETTI

illustrated by HOLLY MEADE

CANDLEWICK PRESS

First edition 2011

Library of Congress Cataloging-in-Publication Data

Bartoletti, Susan Campbell.
Naamah and the ark at night / Susan Campbell Bartoletti ; illustrated by Holly Meade. — 1st U.S. ed.
p. cm.
ISBN 978-0-7636-4242-6
[1. Stories in rhyme. 2. Noah's ark — Fiction. 3. Noah's wife (Biblical figure) — Fiction.
4. Animals — Fiction. 5. Night — Fiction. 6. Lullabies.] I. Meade, Holly, ill. II. Title.

PZ8.3.B2545Nab 2011
[E] — dc22   2010040398

11 12 13 14 15 16 SWT 10 9 8 7 6 5 4 3 2 1

Printed in Dongguan, Guangdong, China

This book was typeset in Rialto Piccolo.
The illustrations were done in watercolor collage.

Candlewick Press
99 Dover Street
Somerville, Massachusetts 02144

visit us at www.candlewick.com

For Rocco and Alia, who came two by two,
and Mia, who came by one
S. C. B.

As rain falls over the ark at night,

As water swirls in the dark of night,

As thunder crashes the seams of night,

As Noah tosses in dreams of night,

As restless animals prowl at night,

As they pace and roar and growl at night,

Naamah sings all through the night.

She sings and strokes their hair at night;

She sings a bedtime prayer at night.

She sings for moon to fill the night;

She sings for stars to thrill the night.

She sings for earth and sky at night,

Soothes her sons and their wives at night;

Naamah sings all through the night.

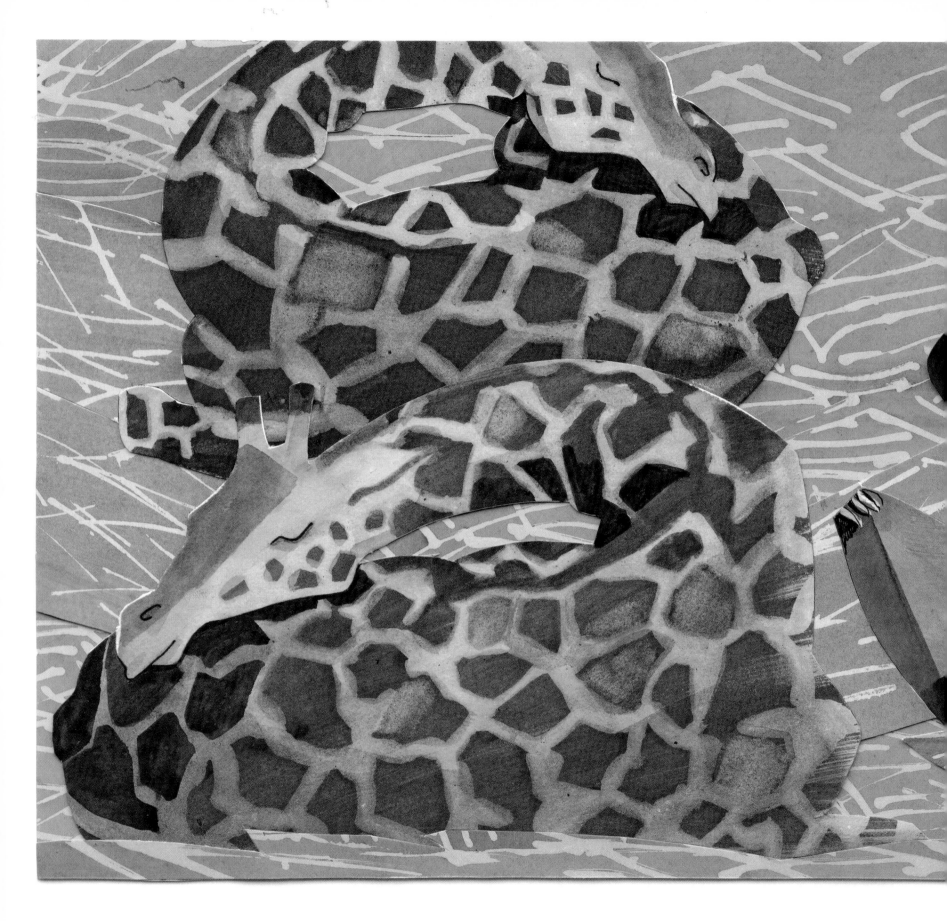

Over the ark, song flows at night.

Two by two, eyes close at night.

Two by two, wings furl at night.

Two by two, tails curl at night.

Two by two, the beasts of night

Are lullabied to sleep at night.

Naamah sings all through the night.

Beneath the clouds that shroud the night,

The ark sails long into the night,

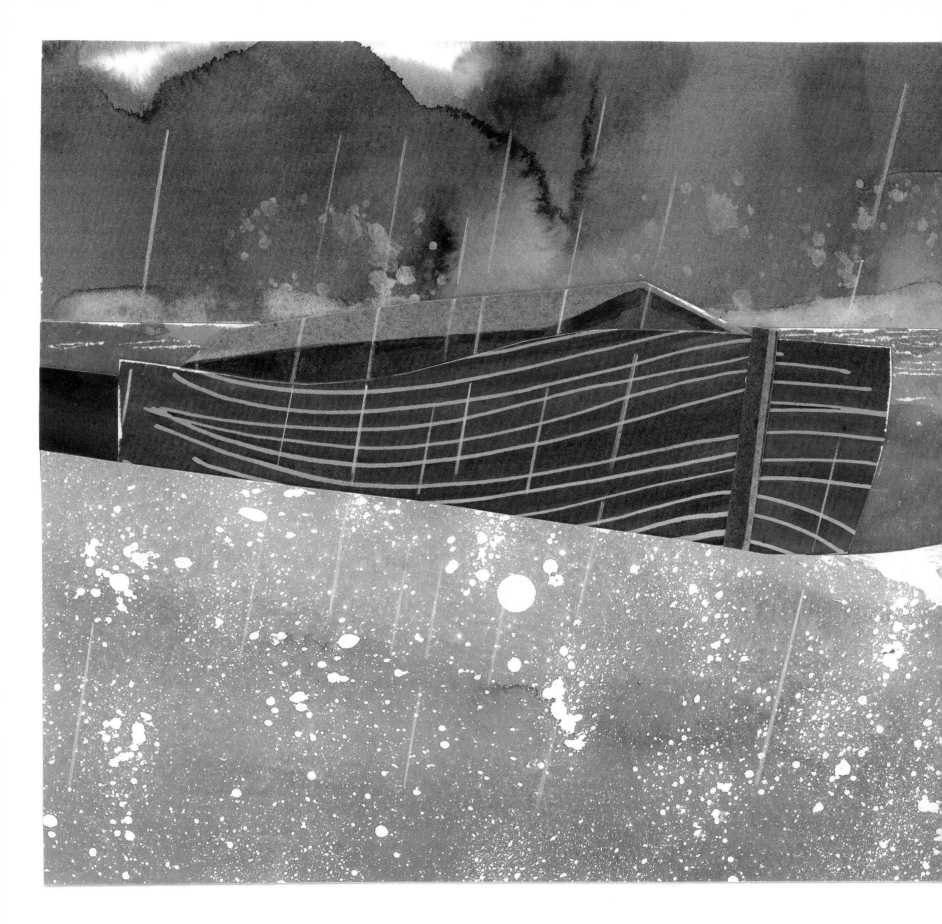

Cradled by the song of night.

Hush hush hush, good night.

Author's Note

As a little girl, when I visited my grandmother, I played with a wooden Noah's ark. I lined up the animals, two by two, and boarded them safely. I imagined the falling rain. I imagined the rising floodwaters. I imagined the ark tossing and turning on the churning sea.

That ark now sits on a shelf in my dining room. All grown up, I no longer play with the ark. I dust it. And as I do, I find that my imagination turns to Noah's wife. In the book of Genesis, we're told that Noah was a just man, full of grace. But what kind of woman was his wife?

The answer may lie in her name. Although an American scholar named Francis Utley listed 103 possible names for Noah's wife in 1941, some rabbinical legends tell us that Noah's wife was called Naamah because her deeds were pleasant. These legends also tell of another Naamah whose name meant "great singer." The name, a variation of the name Naomi (which means "sweet" or "pleasant") is usually given three syllables (Na-ah-mah or Nay-ah-mah).

I like these interpretations of her name. They help me imagine how she inspired and comforted Noah and their three sons and their wives, as well as all the animals. Perhaps Naamah sang.

The form of *Naamah and the Ark at Night* was inspired by a poetic structure called a *ghazal* (sounds like "guzzle"). The *ghazal* is a very old and extremely disciplined Arabic form, dating back to at least the seventh century. Its strict form, usually used in poems about longing and love and loss, requires each couplet to end in the same word, preceded by a rhyming word. An Internet search will help you find more information about the traditional *ghazal*. I thank poet and friend Molly Peacock for introducing me to this form with her sonnet-*ghazal*, "Of Night."

Over the years, Western poets have taken liberty with the traditional *ghazal* form, as I have with *Naamah and the Ark at Night*, a lullaby that I hope inspires readers to trust in the darkness, as Naamah did.